THE PUPPY PLACE

BIGGIE

THE PUPPY PLACE

Don't miss any of these other stories by Ellen Miles!

THE PUPPY PLACE

BIGGIE

ELLEN
MILES

SCHOLASTIC INC.

ISBN 978-1-338-68696-8

10 9 8 7 6 5 4 3 2 1   20 21 22 23 22

Printed in the U.S.A.   40
First printing 2020

CHAPTER ONE

Lizzie Peterson trudged along the sidewalk, feeling her backpack thump against her shoulders. It was a cloudy, gray afternoon in September. The leaves on the trees that lined her street hadn't changed color yet, but you couldn't say they were bright green, either. Their dullness seemed to match her mood.

"What's the matter, Lizzie?" her mom asked, when Lizzie arrived home from school.

Lizzie shrugged as she bent down to give her puppy, Buddy, a scritch between the ears. He gazed up at her, his brown eyes shining with happiness, love, and excitement. She couldn't help smiling back at him. Dogs always made her feel better. They had a great attitude, upbeat and ready for anything. At least, Buddy did. He was the best puppy ever, and Lizzie knew how lucky she was that he was part of her family. She reached down to stroke the heart-shaped white patch on Buddy's chest.

"I'm just bored, I guess," she said to her mom. "It's been a while since anything exciting happened."

Mom gave Lizzie a hug, then held her by the shoulders and looked her straight in the eye, smiling. "You mean, since we had a new puppy to foster?" she asked.

Lizzie kicked her sneaker against the floor. Mom always seemed to be able to see straight into her heart. "Maybe," she said. As usual, Mom was right.

The Petersons were a foster family who helped

puppies who needed homes. Some puppies had stayed with them for only days while others were there for weeks. Only one, Buddy, had stayed forever. Lizzie's family (her parents; her younger brother, Charles; and their toddler brother, the Bean) had fostered golden retrievers and a Great Dane plus practically every other common breed, as well as mutts large and small. Sometimes Lizzie couldn't believe her good luck.

Lizzie had a "Dog Breeds of the World" poster hanging on her bedroom wall, and she loved to draw a red heart next to every breed she'd met or fostered. She'd still never even seen one of those hairless dogs, the Chinese crested, but she was sure she would one of these days.

Mom nodded. "Having a new puppy is always exciting," she said. "Don't worry, one always comes along just when you least expect it."

Lizzie gave Buddy one more pat. Then she hung

her blue school backpack on a hook by the door and grabbed the green one from the next hook. This was her dog-walking backpack, equipped with a variety of yummy treats, extra leashes and harnesses, and poop bags. "I'd better get going," she said. It was time for work. Lizzie and her best friend, Maria, (and their two friends, Briana and Daphne) had a very successful dog-walking business, with many happy clients (dogs and people). They were successful because they all loved dogs, and also because they all knew at least a little bit about dog training (Lizzie knew a lot). But the main reason for their success? They were responsible. Lizzie had never once missed a walk, and neither had her friends. They had a perfect record, and all their clients definitely appreciated that.

Lizzie kissed Buddy once more, then stood up tall and stretched. She put on the green backpack.

"Okay," she told Mom. "See you later!" She waved as she headed down the front steps.

As she walked, Lizzie thought about other breeds she hadn't met yet. Like a borzoi, a sleek runner with an elegant, swooping chest. Or a big white komondor, a brave protector of sheep with a long, thick coat. She'd never even met a Vizsla, or a Norwegian elkhound. But she would. No matter what it took. It was Lizzie's main goal in life to "heart" every dog on her poster.

Lizzie was headed to see her first client, a young German shepherd named Tank. Tank was big and all muscle, but he was the sweetest, most gentle dog. He wouldn't hurt a fly, even if it landed right on his soft brown nose. Lizzie had brought a pocketful of Tank's favorite treats along (freeze-dried liver), since she planned to work on his leash-walking skills today. She reached in to check that the little brown chunks were there.

They were. Good. It was never much use trying to teach dogs if you didn't have excellent treats to offer them.

After Tank, and four other dogs, Lizzie was looking forward to walking her favorite new client: Domino, a peppy little Jack Russell. He was white with black spots, including one near his tail that was the exact shape and size of a domino. He was the happiest dog she'd ever met, and still full of energy even though he was seven years old. Domino was bursting with charm, and being around him never failed to cheer Lizzie up.

The Jacksons, Domino's family, were super sweet. Lizzie knew that when their young twins, Jenny and Merrie, got a little older, they would love taking Domino for walks. For now, while the twins were still babies, Mrs. and Mr. Jackson needed help. They adored Domino, but since the kids had come they didn't always have time during the week to give him the exercise and attention he needed.

"Lizzie!" said Mrs. Jackson when she opened the door later that afternoon. "So great to see you. Domino's been off-the-wall excited today, and super hyper." She held a baby in each arm as the little black-and-white pup did figure eights around her feet.

Lizzie dropped to her knees to give Domino a hug. He wriggled in and out of her arms, then spun around in a circle, barking happily. He dashed down the hall, toenails scrabbling, and came prancing back with a giant neon-green alien stuffie. He bit down on it to make it squeak, then tossed it into the air.

Yay, you're here! Let's play!

Lizzie laughed. "He always gets this way by Friday," she said. "Then he chills out a little after you hike with him all weekend. He needs adventure in his life."

"Domino does love going on adventures," Mrs. Jackson told Lizzie. "He's been on every high peak in this state and a few others. He's run races, he's ridden down crazy rapids in a red canoe, and he loves to bound through the snow when my husband and I go cross-country skiing."

Mr. and Mrs. Jackson were both tall and lean, and always seemed to be dressed in sleek black athletic clothes, with special zippers and reflective stripes. The twins went along on all the hikes and runs and ski trips, carried in special sporty backpacks or strapped into fancy strollers.

After she finished walking Domino, Lizzie headed for home. As usual, she was feeling much happier now that she had spent some time with the frisky pup—and all the other dogs.

But she was about to get even happier.

Mom met her at the door. She had a huge smile on her face. "Remember what I said before?" she asked. "About a new foster puppy coming along when you least expect it?"

Lizzie nodded, curious. Her mom grinned as she held up her car keys and gave them a shake so they tinkled like chimes. "Ready to go pick up our new puppy?"

CHAPTER TWO

"Yay!" yelled Lizzie. "A new puppy." Then she paused. "Wait a second." She folded her arms, cocked her head, and looked her mother right in the eye. "Did you know about this before?"

"No!" said her mom, holding up her hands. Then she grinned. "Well, sort of no. I had an inkling. An idea. I mean, I knew it was maybe sort of possibly a possibility." She was laughing, and Lizzie had to laugh, too.

"Honestly?" her mom went on, when she'd caught her breath. "I guess I did know. I just didn't want to tell all of you until I was positive it was going to happen. I didn't want to disappoint you and your brothers."

"Do Charles and the Bean know yet?" Lizzie asked.

Her mom shook her head. "For now it's just between us. Your dad knows, of course. I wouldn't do this without checking with him."

That was pretty much the Peterson family rule when it came to taking in a foster puppy. Both parents had to agree. Of course, the rule had been broken before. There had even been a few times when neither parent even knew there was going to be a new pup in the house until it was too late.

"So what are we waiting for?" Lizzie asked her mom. "Let's go get"—she stopped and raised her eyebrows—"um, what's his or her name?"

Her mom started to laugh again. "You won't

believe it. His name is"—she could hardly get it out—"Biggie!"

Lizzie cracked up, too. "So, he's a big dog?" she asked, imagining another Saint Bernard or a Great Dane, or maybe that komondor she hadn't met yet.

"Nope," said Mom. "Although I've heard that he thinks he is. He's a Yorkie."

Lizzie stopped laughing. "Oh, no. Like Princess?" she asked. She had never been a fan of small dogs, although the Petersons had fostered some wonderful ones that had helped to change her mind. She could admit that not every small dog was yappy and obnoxious. But Princess! Princess had been quite the spoiled handful, and Lizzie was not in the mood to cater to a pampered puppy's every whim.

"No, no," said Mom. "Biggie isn't like that at all. Come on, I'll tell you all about it while we drive."

Once they were in the car, Lizzie's mom started the story. "You know Estelle from the newspaper?"

Lizzie had met Estelle. She was a photographer who worked with Mom on a lot of articles and was always striding up to their front door with a bunch of cameras around her neck.

"Yes, you worked with her on that parade story. She took all those great photos of the floats," Lizzie said.

"Right! Well, she has a daughter, Tamara, who is just out of college. Tamara and her roommates thought it would be fun to have a dog, like a kind of a mascot," Mom explained, as she drove. "They got Biggie this summer. Estelle says they all love him, but they've realized that they are all way too busy with their jobs and other activities. Biggie was getting left home alone too much, and that wasn't working out so well."

Lizzie nodded. She could just imagine. A

bored and lonely puppy was not always a well-behaved puppy. "Let me guess. Barking all day and bothering the neighbors?" she asked. "Being destructive? Maybe even peeing in the house?"

"Check, check, and check," Mom said, smiling into the rearview mirror at Lizzie. "You guessed it. Estelle said it's been a very hard decision for the girls, but they're sure now that they really can't keep Biggie. While you were out walking dogs, Tamara called me to confirm that we'd take him." She pulled the car into the driveway of a yellow house with a big front porch. "Here we are," she said.

Lizzie climbed out of the car. Immediately, a little dog jumped off the porch and charged toward her, barking in a high-pitched voice.

Hey, you! What are you doing here?! Better watch out, I'm ferocious!

Lizzie laughed. "Hi, Biggie," she said. Biggie was a sturdy, scruffy-looking dude with wiry hair that stuck up in spikes from the top of his head. His bushy eyebrows stuck out, too, over little black eyes that glittered with energy. His tiny tail wagged at double speed as he barked.

"Hey, Mr. Tough Guy," Lizzie said, crouching down to open her arms up to the little pup. Lizzie knew how to speak Dog. She could tell by Biggie's body language that, for all his noise, he wasn't going to hurt anyone. That wagging tail gave him away.

"Biggie!" a girl called from the porch. She came running down the brick walkway, blond braids bouncing. "Bad boy. You be quiet now, hear?" She scooped him up into her arms and nuzzled the top of his head.

"You must be Tamara," said Lizzie's mom. She introduced herself and Lizzie.

"Nice to meet you," said Tamara. But she didn't look happy. She buried her face in Biggie's fur, and when she looked back up, Lizzie saw that she had tears in her eyes.

"I know," Mom said gently. "You love him, don't you?"

"We all do," said another girl, who had come out the front door. "Mr. Big is the best." She reached out a hand to pet him. Biggie snuffled at her fingers. "I'm Janice," she said. "Our other roomie, Madison, can't even bring herself to come out to say good-bye. She's inside, crying on the couch."

Mom nodded. "You're doing the right thing, though," she said softly. "When you're all a bit older and more settled, you can have all the pets you want. But maybe right now just isn't the time."

Tamara nodded, sniffed, and looked at Lizzie. "Take good care of him?" she asked, as she put Biggie into Lizzie's arms.

"I promise," said Lizzie. "And we'll find him the best home ever."

At that, Tamara and Janice burst into tears and fell into each other's arms.

"Um, I think we'll be going," Mom said.

Tamara held out a hand and waved, without looking up. Lizzie could tell that she didn't even want to watch Biggie go. Poor Tamara. Poor Janice. Lizzie knew how hard it must be to give up this adorable bundle of energy. She gave Biggie a squeeze, and he licked her cheek. Her heart flipped over with love for him as she inhaled his sweet puppy scent. He might be little, and he might be a handful, but Lizzie already knew that Biggie was a very special pup. "Don't worry," she told him. "You're in good hands."

CHAPTER THREE

The next day, Lizzie and Maria laughed as they watched Biggie sniff at a mailbox, then lift one back leg so high that he almost fell right over. Lizzie knew that male dogs peed that way in order to mark their territory and to warn other dogs to stay out of their way.

Biggie swaggered down the sidewalk, towing Lizzie along behind him while Maria followed. He held his head and tail high, looking from side to side as if expecting challengers to pop out of the bushes. "Biggie McBig," Lizzie said fondly, as they continued their walk. "You really do think you're the king of the hill, don't you?"

I own this place. I don't even really know where I am—but I own this place.

Lizzie giggled. "Isn't he funny?" she asked Maria. It was after school on Friday, and Lizzie and Maria were about to split up to take care of their dog-walking clients, but Lizzie wanted Maria to meet Biggie.

"He likes to act like a tough guy," Lizzie added. "But it truly is just an act. Underneath it all, he's a total love bug."

"I can tell. What a cutie," Maria said.

Biggie had settled in quickly at the Petersons'. He and Buddy had already become best friends who loved to sleep curled up together on Buddy's bed. Biggie was gentle with the Bean, but happy to play boisterous games of tug with Charles. He had won Mom's heart and had spent plenty of time sitting on her lap, "helping" her knit.

"And Dad already took him down to the fire-house to show him off," Lizzie told Maria now. They watched Biggie scratch the dirt with his back legs to throw it up behind him, making sure his scent spread out as much as possible. "The firefighters gave him a fire hydrant squeaky toy and named him their new mascot."

Everybody loved Biggie.

"He really is a character," said Maria. "I don't see how anybody could stand to give him up."

"I know," said Lizzie. "But Tamara and Janice did the right thing. Can you imagine this dude home alone all day, every day?" She called Biggie over, then reached down to scratch between his ears. He snuffled at her fingers and wagged his tail. "Biggie deserves lots of attention and he needs lots of activity. I took him on three walks yester-day, plus he got to play with a whole bunch of dogs at the dog park and he still wasn't tired."

"How was he with the other dogs? Are you sure he's going to be okay with all your clients today?" Maria asked, as they started to walk again.

"I think he'll be fine," said Lizzie. "He starts out trying to pretend he's the boss, but he really just wants to play." Usually she tried to walk foster puppies separately, since she felt that her clients deserved her full attention. But Biggie really did seem to get along with every other dog he met, and he definitely needed all the exercise she could give him. "I can't wait for him to meet Domino. I think the two of them will really hit it off."

When they got to the corner of Maple and Spring, Lizzie and Maria said good-bye and headed their own ways. "Now, you be good," Lizzie told Biggie, as she walked him up to Tank's house. "Tank is a big dude, but the truth is I think he's a tiny bit scared of smaller dogs."

Biggie looked up at her, cocking his head.

Who are you calling small? Just kidding. I'll be good.

He wagged his tail and blinked at Lizzie, almost as if he were giving her a wink.

"Good boy," said Lizzie. She tightened her hold on his leash as she opened the door.

Tank, who was always happy to see her, rushed toward Lizzie. He stopped in his tracks when he saw Biggie. The little pup was standing tall—as tall as he could manage—next to Lizzie, with his chest pushed out as if to say, "Don't mess with me."

"Biggie," Lizzie said, as a warning. "Be nice."

Biggie wagged his tail and went into a play bow.

No worries, friend. Let's have a good time!

Tank inched forward and the two touched noses. Tank's tail also began to wag. "Good," said

Lizzie. "I knew you could be friends." She clipped Tank's leash to his collar and headed out the door. The two dogs towed her along the sidewalk, roving from side to side as they sniffed, peed, sniffed again, and peed again.

The same routine happened with all the other dogs Lizzie walked that afternoon. Biggie came on strong at first, but in the end everybody was his best friend. "Almost done," she told him, as they headed for Domino's house. "I saved the best for last. And the Jacksons have a fenced yard like we do, so you and Domino can run and chase each other and burn off some extra energy."

She headed up the walk, hoping that the Jacksons were home. She knew they would enjoy meeting Biggie. When she knocked, Mrs. Jackson opened the door almost at once. "Lizzie!" she said. Then she glanced down at Biggie and her face fell. "Oh," she said.

"I—I'm sorry," Lizzie felt terrible. "I don't usually bring our foster dogs along, but I thought—um—" she peered around Mrs. Jackson. Usually Domino would have been right at her owner's heels, excited to see who was at the door. "Where's Domino?"

Mrs. Jackson sighed as she opened the door and ushered Lizzie and Biggie inside. Now Lizzie could see that Mrs. Jackson's eyes were red and puffy. Her hair was mussed and she looked exhausted. "For a second I thought you might know. I thought you might have found him, and brought him home to us," she said. She plopped down on the couch and slumped over, looking as if she was going to cry. "Oh, Lizzie," she said. "Our little Domino is lost."

CHAPTER FOUR

Lizzie gasped. "Oh, no!" she said. "Where? When? How long has he been gone?"

Mr. Jackson had come into the room by then. He sat down next to his wife, putting his arm around her. He looked exhausted, too.

Lizzie was shocked. She had never seen the Jacksons like this before. They were always so energetic, so upbeat.

Mr. Jackson heaved a huge sigh. "It's my fault," he said. "I remember noticing that his collar was loose, but I forgot to tighten it before we headed out on a hike yesterday after work. He must have seen a squirrel or something: he got so excited.

He was jumping up and down and barking and pulling on the leash. Somehow he managed to slip out of his collar and he took off after whatever it was, straight into the underbrush. I called him and called, but—he just disappeared so quickly." Mr. Jackson's voice sounded thick, and Lizzie saw that his eyes were shiny with tears. "I never thought our little guy would take off like that," he finished. He shook his head.

"We were up on the Skyline Trail," said Mrs. Jackson. "You know, the one with the good views? Domino loves that trail. It's his favorite." She wiped her eyes, sniffing.

"We've hiked there so many times," said Mr. Jackson. It was like they had to tell it over and over again. Lizzie had the feeling they'd already told each other the whole story many times. "But he saw a squirrel and he was gone like that"—he snapped his fingers—"before I could even call his name. I was sure he would circle back in a few minutes, or that we'd find him waiting at the car—but there was no sign of him. We hiked up and down the trail all morning, calling his name. Nothing. He wasn't anywhere on the trail, he wasn't in the parking area, he just"—he snapped his fingers again—"disappeared."

Lizzie felt tears spring to her eyes, thinking about how terrible she would feel if Buddy vanished like that. But she just nodded, trying not to make things any worse by breaking down and crying. "And now he's been out there all night?" she asked.

Mr. Jackson put his head in his hands. "I went back out with my headlamp and ran the whole trail at midnight, calling his name. Nothing. Same thing this morning. Where could he have gone?"

Lizzie gripped the arms of her chair. She didn't even want to think about all the things that could happen to a little dog—even one as spunky as Domino—out in the wild.

"We don't know what to do next," said Mrs. Jackson, shaking her head. "We're just—so tired and sad. The twins are upset, too. They're only babies, but they know something isn't right. They're napping now. We're all exhausted."

Lizzie nodded, her thoughts in a whirl. She could tell that the Jacksons were too overwhelmed to be able to think straight. Her first thought was to run home and ask Mom what to do, or call her aunt Amanda, who knew everything about dogs. She needed a grown-up's help—didn't she?

Then Lizzie took a deep breath and tried to focus. She had learned a lot about finding lost dogs when one of her family's foster puppies, a dachshund named Ziggy, had run away. There were things you could do—things besides just looking

28

for the dog yourself. Lots of people panicked when their dog was lost, and just kept searching and searching, without stopping to think.

"The important thing is to spread the word," she told the Jacksons. "You're only two people. But there are plenty of others who will want to help if they know Domino is missing. The more people out there looking, the better our chances are of finding him. And we need to get everybody looking soon—the sooner the better."

Mr. Jackson looked at Lizzie, his brow furrowed. He nodded. "I can see how that would make sense," he said.

Lizzie nodded. "And you have to stay hopeful. Lots of lost dogs are found, or turn up on their own."

"Really?" asked Mrs. Jackson. She sat up straighter.

"Absolutely," said Lizzie, feeling more confident by the minute. They could do this. They could find Domino. She felt it in her bones.

"There's a lot to do," Lizzie went on, holding up a hand to tick things off on her fingers. It was all coming back to her now. "The first thing is to make a poster to hang up in as many places as we can. You should spread the word on social media, and there are some phone calls to make, to shelters and pet stores and the police. And of course we'll keep looking for Domino ourselves."

Mrs. Jackson slumped back in her seat. Lizzie understood. She knew it all sounded like a lot.

"My friends and I can help," she promised. "And I'll talk to my aunt and to Ms. Dobbins, too. They may have some ideas."

Lizzie's aunt Amanda ran a doggy day care, and she helped with things like this all of the time. And Ms. Dobbins was the director of

Caring Paws, the animal shelter where Lizzie volunteered every week. The Jacksons knew Ms. Dobbins because they had adopted Domino from her shelter.

Mrs. Jackson sniffled, then reached for a tissue and blew her nose. "Thank you, Lizzie. I know you love Domino, too."

Just then, Biggie let out a little whine. "Oh, Biggie!" said Lizzie. She had almost forgotten he was there! What a good boy he was. He seemed to understand that something important was happening. Ever since they'd all sat down, he had been lying patiently at Lizzie's feet. Now he stood up, shook himself, and put a paw on her leg.

Is everything okay?

"This is Biggie, our new foster pup," Lizzie told Mr. and Mrs. Jackson, as she pulled the scruffy pup onto her lap. "I hope it's okay that I brought him."

Mrs. Jackson had pulled a pad of paper and a pen out of a drawer in the coffee table. She hunched over it, scribbling things down, making a list. She waved a hand, barely glancing at Biggie.

"It's fine," said Mr. Jackson, as he put his hands on his knees and stood up.

Lizzie could see that the Jacksons were ready to get to work. So was she. "Can you find me a recent picture of Domino?" she asked. "Let's get going on that poster."

CHAPTER FIVE

"There we go," Lizzie said to Biggie, as she stepped back from a telephone pole. She had to admit that the poster looked really good. She had taken a bunch of them with her when she left the Jacksons and was putting a few up on her way home for dinner. Mrs. Jackson had run off about twenty-five posters on her home printer, for starters.

LOST DOG, the poster said at the top, in very big letters. Lizzie and Mr. Jackson had looked up "lost dog poster" online and had found a website that had listed all the things the poster should include. First was that big, eye-catching headline.

Then, underneath, in smaller type, it said, HAVE YOU SEEN DOMINO?

Beneath the words was a picture—sharp, and in color—of a black-and-white dog with a small, square black patch near his tail—a patch the exact size and shape of a domino. In the picture, Domino stood on a flat rock on the edge of a glassy, still lake ringed by tall pine trees. The picture had caught him perfectly: in it he held his nose up to sniff the wind, while his half-flopped ears fluttered in the breeze. His eyes were closed in pure happiness, and he almost seemed to have a smile on his face.

Domino is a male Jack Russell terrier, seven years old, the text said beneath the picture. The website had said to make sure to list all of that information. *He ran off during a hike on the Skyline Drive on September 21, at about 5:30 p.m.* Lizzie felt her heart flip once again when she read those words. "I just still can't believe he's missing," she said to Biggie now, as they headed to the next telephone pole.

The poster listed a phone number for the Jacksons. *Call anytime!* it said. REWARD! The website had said to mention a reward, but without saying how much.

Finally, in big letters across the bottom, it said DO NOT CHASE. Lizzie knew that it was never a good idea to chase a loose dog. Many dogs thought it was a game. Others might be frightened. Either way, chasing a dog usually just made it run away from you.

First thing tomorrow, Mrs. Jackson was going to have 500 more copies made so they could stick them up all over. Mr. Jackson was also going to paint a big version of the sign on plywood, and set it up near the parking area at the Skyline Trail. Both ideas were also suggested by the website.

Lizzie felt almost as exhausted as the Jacksons by the time she got home. She couldn't believe that Mr. Jackson was planning to hike the trail one more time before it got totally dark. They had read that the best time to look for a runaway dog was at dusk and dawn, since he would likely be most active then. "It's not like I can eat or sleep anyway," said Mr. Jackson. "I might as well be out there looking for our little guy."

The next morning, Lizzie woke to Biggie standing over her, licking her face.

Come on! Get up! We have a lot to do!

Lizzie groaned and pushed him away. "Forget it, Biggie. It's Saturday!" She wanted to sleep a little more. Then she remembered. Domino was missing. Maria was coming over early so they could search some more and put up posters. She sat straight up in bed, then threw off the covers and raced downstairs to find her mom. "Any news?" she asked, as she ran into the kitchen.

Her mom was spooning ground coffee into the coffee maker and chatting with Maria, who was already there. "Good morning to you, too," she said. Then she gave Lizzie a hug. "No messages. I'm sorry."

The Jacksons had promised to let Lizzie know the minute they heard anything.

Lizzie sighed.

"I know," said her mom, squeezing her close again. "I really feel bad for the Jacksons. I'm glad it's a weekend so we can do everything we can to help today. First, though, I think you'd better let Biggie and Buddy out to play."

"Let's get these little guys outside," Maria said.

After watching Buddy and Biggie run around,

Lizzie and Maria walked through the neighborhood, putting up signs everywhere. They went downtown, too, and asked all the shopkeepers to put signs in their windows. Briana and Daphne put up posters, too.

Later on, Mom was going to take Lizzie to Caring Paws. Saturday was Lizzie's usual volunteer day anyway, and she wanted to talk to Ms. Dobbins about any other things they could do to help find Domino. Plus, she planned to personally check out every single dog in the shelter. What if someone had brought Domino there? It could be busy at the shelter, and one of the volunteers might have missed hearing about the lost pup.

When Lizzie left them the night before, the Jacksons had been much less gloomy and much more determined to do everything they could to find Domino. "Thanks for getting us on the right track. I just don't know what I'd do without Domino," Mrs. Jackson had said right before Lizzie had left. "The house feels so empty without him. He's a little dog, but he has a big presence."

Lizzie looked at Biggie walking along beside her. She had brought him along while they put up posters. "Domino is just like you," she said. "He's a big dog in a little dog's body."

Biggie wagged his tail and gave her a doggy grin as he strutted along.

That's me! Don't forget, I'm the boss around here.

Lizzie and Maria were on Maple Street, stapling up posters, when they heard a car horn beeping behind them. It was Mom. She pulled over and hopped out of the car. "Mrs. Jackson just texted me," she told the girls. "They had a call from someone who might have seen Domino just now, up on the Skyline Trail."

"What are we waiting for?" Lizzie asked. She scooped Biggie into her arms and headed for the car. "Let's go."

CHAPTER SIX

"Who called?" Lizzie asked, as she fastened her seat belt and pulled Biggie onto her lap. "What did they say? Where exactly on the trail did they see Domino? Are the Jacksons already at the trail?"

Mom held up a hand. "Hold on there, buckaroo. That's a lot of questions all at once, and to tell you the truth, I have no answers. All I know is what I told you: somebody texted Mrs. Jackson that they saw Domino on the trail. That's all. We'll find out more when we get there."

Lizzie sat back and let out a breath.

Maria reached over to take her hand. "We'll find him," she said. "Don't worry."

Lizzie shook her head. "You don't know that," she said. Even though she was doing her best to be optimistic, Lizzie *did* worry. Domino was such a little guy. What if a coyote had grabbed him, or what if he was sick or injured? Domino was also very cute, the kind of dog that everyone fell in love with at first sight. What if someone had dognapped him and had already driven miles and miles away? What if he had run out into the road and—

Lizzie put her face in her hands. She knew it didn't do any good to think these kind of thoughts, but it was hard to keep them out of her head. The night before she had tossed and turned in bed for a long time, thinking about Domino out there in the world, all by himself.

Maria was right. They would find him. They

absolutely *had* to find him. And it was a very good sign that someone might have spotted him. Lizzie shook herself and sat up straight. She had to stay positive! She hugged Biggie closer and kissed the top of his head. His fur was so wiry that it tickled her nose until she had to sneeze. The sneeze made her giggle and hug Biggie again. He licked her cheek and wagged his funny little feathery tail.

Hang in there. Everything's going to be okay. Biggie's here!

Lizzie laughed. She could tell that Biggie wanted to help. He sensed that she was upset, and he'd found a way to cheer her up—so he already had helped. "You're right," she told Maria, reaching out to squeeze her friend's hand. "We'll find Domino. Let's stay positive. After all, somebody just spotted him, right?"

When Mom pulled into the parking lot at the start of the Skyline Trail, Lizzie saw a small crowd of people milling around near a black SUV. That was the Jacksons' car! Lizzie jumped out, still carrying Biggie in her arms, as soon as Mom pulled to a stop. She charged toward the group and saw Mr. Jackson, dressed in his usual sporty clothes, standing with his hands on his hips as he spoke to the people who had come to help. It seemed that they had all seen flyers and wanted to help find Domino.

"I can't thank you all enough for coming out," he said. "The more eyes we have out there the better." He handed out flyers to everyone. "I know most of you have seen this—that's why you're here—but I figured you might as well have one with you. We just had news that Domino—or a dog that looks a lot like him—was just spotted about a mile up the trail, near the second waterfall."

Somebody cheered. "Thanks," said Mr. Jackson. "It makes me happy, too. But we still have to find Domino. Does everyone have some treats to offer him, if you see him?"

A few people shook their heads. Lizzie came up next to Mr. Jackson. "I have plenty," she said, holding up a bag she'd pulled out of her jacket pocket. She put Biggie down on the ground, then gave out handfuls of treats to everyone who needed them.

"The biggest thing is, don't chase him," Mr. Jackson went on. "If anybody runs toward him, he'll probably just get spooked and take off deeper into the woods. Domino is hard to catch on the best days, and after spending a night out here on his own, he's probably pretty freaked out."

"Should we call his name while we hike?" a woman in a red knit hat asked.

Mr. Jackson looked blank for a moment. He

glanced down at Lizzie, eyebrows raised. Lizzie was ready. She had been researching everything she could about finding lost dogs. "Some people say yes," she told the woman. "Others say no, that even after one night in the woods, some dogs get a little wild and kind of forget who they are. But I don't think it can hurt. Just call in a gentle, friendly voice so you don't scare him."

"I brought a squeaky toy that my dog loves," said a man who seemed to know Mr. Jackson. He held up a pink unicorn and gave it a squeeze.

"Great idea!" said Lizzie. "It might grab Domino's attention."

It had certainly grabbed Biggie's. He tugged his leash out of Lizzie's hands and ran toward the man with the toy.

Gimme that! I'll take care of it. That's my department.

"Biggie, no!" said Lizzie, grabbing the leash that was trailing behind him along the ground. She looked at Mr. Jackson and shrugged. "Maybe I shouldn't have brought him, but we rushed right over."

"It's fine," said Mr. Jackson. Again, he seemed to ignore Biggie. He clapped his hands. "Okay, let's head out," he said. "You all have my cell phone number—it's on the poster. Please call if you see or hear anything at all."

Lizzie and Biggie headed up the trail with Mr. Jackson, while Mom and Maria followed behind. At first, Lizzie jogged to keep up with Mr. Jackson's long, fast stride. Finally, out of breath, she had to slow down. She watched as he disappeared up the trail. That man was focused on one thing and one thing only: finding Domino.

"Walk with us, Lizzie," said Mom, putting an arm around her.

"Yeah, walk with us, Biggie," said Maria, reaching down to give his scruffy head a pat. "Maybe Biggie can help find Domino. He's a dog, right? With a dog sense of smell?"

Lizzie knew what Maria was talking about. They'd both learned that dogs have a sense of smell that is about 10,000 times better than a human's. Lizzie had even read that sometimes bloodhounds were used to find lost dogs. If anybody could sniff out Domino, it would be another dog. "Right," said Lizzie. "C'mon, Biggie, let's find Domino. I know you guys would love each other."

As if he understood, Biggie put his nose to the ground and began to zig and zag his way up the trail.

I'll do my best! Unless I get distracted by a—

Just then a squirrel ran across the trail up ahead, and Biggie nearly pulled Lizzie's arm off as he tried to charge after it. Maybe using a dog to find a dog wasn't the best idea after all.

CHAPTER SEVEN

Hours later, as the afternoon began to grow late and the sky turned dusky, Lizzie and Maria stood in the parking lot, back at the beginning of the trail. Mom and a very dejected-looking Mr. Jackson were talking with another woman, over by the Petersons' car.

"I can't believe we didn't see or hear a thing," Lizzie said. They had hiked and hiked, all the way up the steep trail to the top of Eastman Mountain, where there was a broad view of the farmland, rivers, and valleys below. The whole way up and back Lizzie had kept her eyes peeled, swinging her gaze from side to side, peering deep into the tangled woods. She had totally expected to glimpse a flash of black and white, or hear snuffling or whining. "I just know he's somewhere out here."

Her voice was raspy from calling Domino's name, over and over. Her legs were tired, and she was hungry and thirsty. She felt exhausted, and sad. They had looked so hard and hiked so far, all for nothing. Domino was nowhere to be seen.

Biggie pawed her leg, and when she looked down at him, he stared back up at her, cocking his head and seeming to raise his bushy eyebrows.

What about me? I did my best!

"Oh, you were a big help, Biggie," said Lizzie, crouching down to pet him. "I know you tried. You sniffed every rock and every bush and every tree and every root and—" She broke off and scratched him between the ears, feeling as if she might cry. Night was falling, and Domino, poor little Domino, was still out there somewhere. There was nobody to talk to him, nobody to pet him, nobody to scratch him between the ears. Instead there was only cold, and darkness, and maybe even scary wild animals like coyotes or bears.

Lizzie stood up and peered into the woods one more time. Maybe they should do the whole hike over again, before it got completely dark. Most of the other searchers had already gone home, but Lizzie—as tired as she felt—wasn't ready to give up. She couldn't bear to think of the frightened little dog out here all by himself.

"We'll find him," Maria said. But she didn't sound a hundred percent sure. In fact, Lizzie could tell that her friend was feeling almost as hopeless as she was. "We can put up more signs,"

Maria went on. "Maybe make some more phone calls." But she didn't sound excited about it. She sounded as if she felt as exhausted and sad as Lizzie.

Then Mr. Jackson trotted over. "New plan," he said. He seemed energized. "That lady"—he pointed at the woman he and Mom had been talking to—"had some good ideas. She's been through it, lost her dog here last year." He nodded. "And guess what? She found him."

"She did?" Lizzie asked, feeling a flicker of hope in her chest. "Here?"

Mr. Jackson nodded. "She went out to the spot on the trail where she'd last seen him and set up a little bed for him, in a dog crate with the door propped open. She put one of her sweatshirts in it, something that smelled like her, and a toy that he always loved. And a pile of his favorite treats."

Lizzie was nodding. "That makes sense," she

said. She could picture it. Domino couldn't help but be attracted to a setup like that. Any dog would want to check it out. "But how did she know if the dog came by? If the treats were gone they could have just been eaten by another animal."

Mr. Jackson nodded. "Right. But she put a trail cam up, too," said Mr. Jackson.

"A trail cam?" Lizzie asked.

"It's a camera you mount on a tree," Mr. Jackson explained. "It goes off automatically when something moves nearby, even at night. Then it makes a movie of whatever's moving. If it's at night, it takes the movie using special infrared technology."

"Wow," said Maria. "And she saw her dog on the camera?"

"Yes!" Mr. Jackson was practically dancing with excitement. "He came back every few hours to check on the spot, and to eat treats, so she knew he was alive. She could never get there in time to catch him. But finally, after three days, he curled up on the bed and she found him there, fast asleep."

Lizzie couldn't help grinning. How could she have forgotten the most important thing about looking for a lost dog? You had to stay positive. Optimistic. Exactly the way Mr. Jackson seemed after talking to the woman. "It sounds like a fantastic idea," she said. Now she felt energized, too. "Maybe we can bring all that stuff up here tomorrow."

Mr. Jackson raised his eyebrows. "Tomorrow?" He shook his head. "I'm off to buy a camera right now," he said. "Then I'm heading home to pick up all the other stuff: sweatshirts and a bed and everything. Then I'm coming right back up here to set it all up. I'm not going to wait another minute."

Biggie seemed to sense the excitement. He put his paws up on Mr. Jackson's leg and gave him a doggy grin, wagging his tail.

Now you're talking!

This time, Mr. Jackson didn't ignore Biggie. He smiled down at the scruffy pup and knelt to give him some pets. "That's right, pal," he said. "We're gonna find my best friend. We're gonna find Domino."

CHAPTER EIGHT

"Phew!" said Mom, as she, Lizzie, and Maria climbed into her car. "That was quite the hike! I'm ready to collapse on the couch for a while; how about you two?"

Lizzie met her mom's eyes in the rearview mirror. "Um," she said. "Can you drop us at Caring Paws? I want to talk to Ms. Dobbins to see if she has any other suggestions about finding a lost dog. She was really nice about me not coming in for my regular volunteer shift today, but Maria and I still want to at least go visit the dogs and make sure Domino isn't there."

Mom raised her eyebrows. "What about Biggie?" she asked.

"He just had that big hike," said Lizzie. "Even for our little tough guy, that's plenty. He's all tuckered out." She hugged Biggie close and giggled when his wiry eyebrows tickled her cheek. Biggie never failed to make her laugh. He really had a talent for cheering people up. Biggie snuffled Lizzie's neck, then suddenly licked it, making her giggle again. "Biggie!" she said. He gazed up at her, wagging his little tail. His eyebrows twitched as he cocked his head and stuck out his chest.

Yes? That's my name, and everybody knows it. I'm also known as Mr. Big, Biggie McBig, Biggles, Bigglesworth, Biggles McGiggles, and a few dozen other names.

Maria cracked up. "He sure does think he's the cat's pajamas, as my dad would say."

"Or in this case, the dog's pajamas," agreed Mom, from the front seat. She pulled into the parking lot at Caring Paws and turned around to look at Lizzie. "I'm coming back for you two in an hour," she said. "You need to be at home for supper and some downtime. It's been a long day."

"Perfect," said Lizzie, as she and Maria climbed out of the car.

Ms. Dobbins greeted them at the door of the shelter. "Any luck?" she asked. Earlier Lizzie had used Mom's phone to call and tell Ms. Dobbins about the hiker who'd reported seeing Domino.

Lizzie shook her head. "No, but we're staying positive. Mr. Jackson is on his way to buy a trail camera, and he'll set it up tonight."

"They're also going to put out a crate for Domino

to go into, with some of his food and treats and toys and a sweatshirt that Mr. or Mrs. Jackson wore," added Maria.

Ms. Dobbins agreed. "Perfect. I was about to suggest those things. And have they checked the local lost dogs page online?"

"I think so," said Lizzie. "I'll ask them later. Any other ideas?"

Ms. Dobbins thought for a second. "Next time you're out looking for Domino, carry your treats in a crinkly bag, like a foil potato-chip bag. Lots of dogs know what that sound means, and find it irresistible." She smiled.

"Speaking of dogs," said Lizzie, "can we go visit everybody? I just want to be sure that Domino's not here."

"Good idea," said Ms. Dobbins. "We've been very busy here, and things can get missed. I'll come with you."

She led the way to the dog kennels. Lizzie and Maria walked up and down the rows. "Hi, Petey," said Lizzie, as she passed a hound mix on her right. On the left were an older black Lab and a cute little pug mix. "Hey, Junior. Hello there, Sadie."

All the dogs were happy to see Lizzie. Even the shyest ones thumped their tails when she slipped them treats. "Sorry I didn't get to walk all of you today," Lizzie said. "All you good, good dogs." She stopped at a pit bull named Buster's cage and gave him a special scratch beneath his right ear when he pressed up against the fencing. "Yes, you, too, Buster," she said. "You're a good dog, too. Yes you are."

Lizzie was happy to see each of the dogs. But she did not see Domino.

"Tomorrow I'll bring you a new stack of flyers for the front desk," Lizzie told Ms. Dobbins, as she and Maria headed out to the parking lot to meet Mom. "It looks like the ones I gave you are almost gone already."

"Lots of people care about lost dogs," said Ms. Dobbins. "They really want to help."

After dinner that night, Mrs. Jackson called to ask if Lizzie could come over to talk about plans for the next day. "We have a whole list of people who want us to call or email them if we're going to do another search," said Mrs. Jackson. "Plus, Mr. Jackson wants to tell you about setting up the trail camera." She paused and cleared her throat. "And—could you bring that cute little Biggie with you? I think I'm overdue for some dog cuddles."

"What about your downtime?" Mom asked when Lizzie asked for a ride to the Jacksons' house.

"I can't rest, anyway," Lizzie told her. "Not

while Domino is still out there somewhere, lost and afraid."

Mom nodded and reached for her car keys. "That's my Lizzie," she said with a sigh. "How about if I come in with you?" she asked. "We'll just stay for a few minutes. I'm sure the Jacksons are tired, too."

They might have been tired, but they didn't show it. Mr. Jackson paced excitedly up and down the living room as he told them how and where he had set up the crate and trail cam. "It's near where he ran off, next to this beautiful big boulder that he used to like to scramble on top of."

Mrs. Jackson had pulled Biggie into her arms as soon as he'd sauntered into the house. Now she sat holding him on her lap, stroking his scraggly fur as she told Lizzie and her mom about the spreadsheet she was making of people who wanted to help. "I've got their phone numbers in there, and the times they're available—" She broke off into a giggle as Biggie's eyebrows tickled her neck. She looked down at him fondly. "You're not Domino," she told him. "But I have to admit that you're a real cutie, and a character to boot."

That's me!

"Hey, would you like to keep him overnight?" Lizzie asked. Maybe Biggie would be a comfort to the Jacksons. Lizzie had heard about cat cafés, where people who didn't own kitties but loved them could go to sip coffee with a warm cat on their laps. Why couldn't she lend out Biggie?

Mrs. Jackson looked tempted. So did Mr. Jackson—for a moment. Then he shook his head. "Thanks, but we really need to focus all our energy on Domino," he said. Still, he did come over to sit next to his wife and give Biggie a belly rub. Lizzie could tell that having a dog nearby did cheer the Jacksons up a little.

By the time they left, Lizzie and her mom were both energized and ready for another day of searching—after a good rest. The Jacksons were definitely feeling optimistic, and Lizzie was, too. She couldn't wait to see what the trail camera saw out there near the crate with Domino's familiar items.

CHAPTER NINE

"Lizzie, wake up!"

Lizzie groaned and rolled over. Her room was still dark, though she could see a glimmer of light through one window. Why was her mom bothering her so early in the morning? "What," she said, pulling the covers up to her chin. "Why?" She closed her eyes and burrowed her face into her pillow.

"Lizzie, it's about Domino!" Her mother gave Lizzie's shoulder a little shake.

Lizzie sat up and threw off her blankets. "They found him?" she asked.

Biggie, who had been curled up at her side, leapt to his feet and let out a few little barks. He pawed at Lizzie.

Something exciting is happening! Count me in!

"Shh, Biggie," said Mom. "No need to wake up everyone in the house."

"But what happened?" Lizzie asked.

"They didn't find him," said Mom, "but they did see something on the footage from the trail cam. Mrs. Jackson just sent out an email and text blast, hoping for a crew of searchers."

"Let's go," Lizzie said, jumping out of bed. She pulled on a pair of jeans and a favorite old T-shirt that said PLEASE LET ME BE THE PERSON MY DOG THINKS I AM. Then she added a hoodie for warmth against the early morning chill. "I'm ready."

"What about something to eat?" Mom asked, following Lizzie down the stairs.

"I have granola bars in my backpack," said Lizzie. She snapped a leash onto Biggie's collar. "And some dog food. And treats, of course. I'm all set."

Mom held up her hands. "I can see that," she said. She took her car keys off the hook and opened the door. "Let's go, then."

By the time they got to the trailhead parking lot, there were already quite a few people gathered. The news had gotten around quickly.

"Biggie!" someone called from the middle of the crowd, when Lizzie climbed out of the car with Biggie on a leash.

Biggie's head flew up and his ears went forward as he sniffed the air.

I know that voice. I love that voice.

"Mr. Big!" shouted someone else. Then three girls broke out of the group and came zooming over to Biggie.

"Tamara!" said Mom.

Lizzie recognized another one of the other girls. "And Janice," she said. She turned to the third girl. "And you must be Madison. What are you guys doing here?"

The girls were too busy petting Biggie to answer. Tamara had scooped him up into her arms and she held him like a baby while she cooed over him. "Oh, Biggie, we've missed you so much!"

Biggie waggled his eyebrows and licked their cheeks and fingers.

I've missed you, too.

Finally, Tamara turned to Lizzie. "We heard about the lost dog and we wanted to help. We all have Sunday off work, so we got over here as soon as we could. It's a total bonus to see Biggie here!" She paused. "Oh, and you, too, Lizzie and Mrs. Peterson."

The girls insisted on taking turns holding Biggie's leash as the group moved up the trail, a few people at a time so as not to frighten off Domino. Lizzie jogged ahead to catch up with Mr. and Mrs. Jackson. They were moving fast, even though they each had a baby strapped to their front. "What did you see on the trail cam?" Lizzie asked, panting.

"Something," said Mr. Jackson. "Something moved in and out of view, and something took the treats and the food."

"And Domino's favorite toy," added Mrs. Jackson. "Don't forget, Squidly is gone." She smiled at Lizzie. "Domino loves Squidly the squeaky squid."

"Could you tell for sure if it was Domino?" Lizzie asked.

"Well," said Mr. Jackson, swinging his arms as he almost jogged down the trail. "Maybe. It's really hard to tell. The picture is fuzzy, and it was at night. Mostly you see these two glowing eyes, and maybe a pointy nose like Domino's."

"But it had to be him," said Mrs. Jackson. "I just know he's still out here. And I know he wants us to find him." She punched one fist into the other palm. The baby in her carrier stirred and yawned, throwing out one tiny arm. "Oops," said Mrs. Jackson, in a lower voice. "Better not wake Merrie."

Lizzie couldn't keep up with the Jacksons for long, and she soon fell back to hike with Biggie and his adoring girls. They kept exclaiming over him as he roved this way and that across the trail, sniffing at everything.

"Look at him," said Tamara. "Don't you just love his little tail?"

"And his funny little ears!" added Janice. "I've missed those ears sooooo much!"

"My favorite is his tiny paws," Madison said, gazing at the busy pooch at the end of the leash she held.

Biggie stopped for a moment and turned to stare at them.

Quit it with all the "little, tiny" stuff! I'm a big boy. And hold it down. I'm trying to find something here. I need to focus.

Lizzie laughed. Biggie almost looked offended So did Tamara. "Did you see that look?" she asked. "He doesn't like it one bit when we call him 'little.'"

Lizzie nodded, wondering whether there was any chance that Tamara and her friends were thinking about taking Biggie back. They all seemed to love him so much. Could they make it work if they organized their work schedules a bit?

"Can I take a turn holding Biggie?" Lizzie asked. She wanted to walk on her own for a few minutes and think about how to bring up the subject with the girls. A little reluctantly, Tamara passed the pup's leash to Lizzie, and she and her friends headed off up the trail.

"What do you think, Biggie?" Lizzie asked the pup. "Do you want to live with the girls again?"

But the pup wasn't listening. When she looked down at him, Lizzie saw that he was standing very still with his nose up and quivering. His ears twitched and swiveled this way and that.

Hold on there! I think I heard something.

CHAPTER TEN

Lizzie tightened her grip on Biggie's leash. He looked like he was about to bolt into the woods the way he had the day before. In fact, she noticed that they were almost in the same place where that had happened, not far from the big boulder where Mr. Jackson had set up the crate and trail cam. "Easy, there," she said in a soft voice. "Easy, Biggie."

Biggie didn't move. His legs were shaking with excitement, but he didn't move. He stared into the woods, cocking his head this way and that.

Can you hear that? Probably not, with your silly human ears.

Lizzie strained to listen. It was obvious that Biggie could hear something she couldn't. "Okay," she whispered. "Let's go see what it is. But don't drag me through the woods. Let's go slowly. If it's Domino, we don't want to scare him."

She felt a little silly, knowing that Biggie couldn't really understand her words. But somehow he did seem to sense that this was not a time to plunge into the undergrowth. That this was a time to stay calm.

Biggie began to move, threading his way through the trees with Lizzie following. Every so often he would stop to cock his head and listen.

We're getting closer. It's a good thing, too.

Lizzie followed Biggie through the woods, ducking to avoid low branches and stepping carefully over rocks and around roots. "You better not be just chasing a squirrel again," she said to Biggie—but she had a feeling that he was not. This was different. The way Biggie led her, with confidence but without dragging her along, told her that he was after something much more meaningful than a squirrel.

Soon Biggie and Lizzie emerged into a small clearing surrounded by towering pine trees. Lizzie looked around, hoping with all her might to see a small black-and-white dog, but she saw only trees and rocks and—wait, what was that? Biggie pulled her forward, toward a tangle of roots. One of the massive pines must have fallen over in a windstorm. Its base, wider than Lizzie was tall, had pulled straight out of the ground. In a small hollow, where the roots had been, lay Domino, curled up in a tight little ball. His coat was smudged with dirt, but Lizzie knew right away that it was him. She felt tears spring into her eyes.

"Domino," Lizzie said under her breath. She held Biggie's leash tightly as she stepped forward slowly, slowly. The little dog was shivering with cold, and he looked hungry and thin and tired and afraid. As Lizzie and Biggie approached, he held up one white paw as if to say, "Please help me." He looked up at them with big, sad eyes.

Slowly, Lizzie knelt beside him. Biggie joined her, nudging Domino gently with his nose.

Are you okay? I heard you crying.

The scraggly pup lay down next to Domino and curled up beside him as if to warm him.

Lizzie settled next to them and slowly reached out a hand for Domino to sniff. "It's me," she said.

"Lizzie." Domino snuffled weakly at her hand, then let his head drop back to his paws. Lizzie touched him gently, running her hands over his front and back legs, making sure nothing was broken.

"I think you're okay," she said to Domino, when her touch didn't seem to make him flinch. "But you must be so tired, and hungry. Are you ready to go home?" She could just imagine how tuckered out the little dog must be after being on his own for so long. He'd done his best to survive, but now he just needed their help.

Domino raised his head just a little, then nestled in closer against Biggie. Biggie gazed up at Lizzie as he put a protective paw on Domino's shoulder.

He'll be fine. My pal will be just fine.

Just then, Lizzie heard something behind her, and turned to see Mr. Jackson tiptoeing into the clearing. "I knew there was something about this place," he whispered. "I had goose bumps up my back every time I went by it."

"Biggie knew, too," said Lizzie. "He's the one who found Domino."

Mr. Jackson knelt to pet Domino. "Hey, little guy," he said in a low voice. "We're gonna take you home, okay?"

Lizzie felt the tears sliding down her face as Mr. Jackson gently lifted Domino into his arms and held him close. She and Biggie followed him as he carried his beloved pet back to the trail.

By the time they reached the parking lot, most of the search party was already there. Biggie's girls were looking dejected, and Mrs. Jackson was wiping her eyes as she told the group that they might as well take a break until later.

"Look who Biggie found," said Mr. Jackson, as he and Lizzie entered the area.

"Oh!" Mrs. Jackson flew to his side and reached out slowly and gently to pet Domino. Now her tears were flowing freely.

Mom ran over to Lizzie and threw her arms around her. "Good job, sweetie," she whispered into Lizzie's ear.

Lizzie was crying, too. Relief, happiness, exhaustion—it was all mixed together. Biggie put a paw on her leg.

Are you okay?

"I'm fine, Biggie," Lizzie said. "I'm just so glad it's all over and Domino doesn't have to spend another night outside."

Biggie's ears perked up when he heard Domino's name. He tugged on his leash and dragged Lizzie over to where the Jacksons were standing so he could see his new best friend. Biggie put his feet up on Mrs. Jackson's knee and stretched his neck up to sniff at Domino.

Hey, friend.

Mrs. Jackson smiled down at Biggie and gave a little laugh. Then she gave her husband a questioning look. He smiled and nodded.

"What would you think about us adopting Biggie?" Mr. Jackson asked Lizzie. "I've always thought Domino could use a friend to play with, and I have a feeling that Mr. Big here is about the best friend any dog could have."

"Maybe it's the best way to thank him for finding our boy," said Mrs. Jackson. "We promise to give him a great home. It'll be wonderful for Domino to have company when we're off at work."

Lizzie smiled through her tears. She looked over at Tamara and her friends, and saw that they were smiling, too. "Of course," she said. "I can't think of a better home for Biggie."

Domino was found—that was almost enough of a happy ending. But this made it perfect.

PUPPY TIPS

I haven't written about a lost dog since Ziggy, a book about a runaway dachshund. I wanted to write another because, sadly, dogs do sometimes get separated from their owners. It's good to know what to do if your dog ever wanders off. There are lots of websites with tips for finding a lost dog; I used them as I researched this book. There are many steps you can take, from putting up posters to letting people know through social media, to alerting the police and all your local vets and animal shelters. One thing I learned from reading stories about lost dogs is this: don't give up hope! Some dogs who have been gone for days, weeks, and even months eventually find their way home.

Dear Reader,

Thankfully, Zipper has never really run off for long. I would be upset to think of him outside overnight, even though he knows the woods near my house very well. The only time he disappeared for more than a few minutes, it was because he was stuck under the back porch! You can read about that adventure in my Dear Reader notes in the book Kodiak, about a malamute puppy.

Hug your dog, keep her on a leash, and make sure she's wearing a collar with tags at all times. Microchipping your pet is a great idea, too - your parents can talk to a vet about that.

Yours from the Puppy Place,

Ellen Miles

ABOUT THE AUTHOR

Ellen Miles loves dogs, which is why she has a great time writing the Puppy Place books. And guess what? She loves cats, too! (In fact, her very first pet was a beautiful tortoiseshell cat named Jenny.) That's why she came up with the Kitty Corner series. Ellen lives in Vermont and loves to be outdoors with her dog, Zipper, every day, walking, biking, skiing, or swimming, depending on the season. She also loves to read, cook, explore her beautiful state, play with dogs, and hang out with friends and family.

Visit Ellen at ellenmiles.net.

THE PUPPY PLACE

DON'T MISS THE NEXT PUPPY PLACE ADVENTURE!

Here's a peek at Lily

The Petersons had been to Brisco Beach once before. It was so much fun! The town was on a narrow stretch of land that reached out into the ocean. One side had waves—big enough for boogie boarding and surfing. On the other side, the bay side, the water was smooth and calm—good for fishing and swimming. Plus, there was a Main Street where you could get all kinds of treats and souvenirs. There was even a ferry to the main-land, where there were all kinds of other fun things to do. Charles had never done that, and he was hoping to go this year.

"The best part of our last trip was Liberty," Lizzie said. "She was the sweetest puppy."

Dad laughed. "You say that about every puppy." he said.

"But it's true," Lizzie said. "They are all the best."

Charles nodded in agreement. "Lizzie's right," he said. His family fostered puppies. They took care of puppies who needed a home, and they worked to find each puppy its forever family. They loved all of the puppies they had helped. Of course, one puppy really had been the very, very best, and that puppy had become the Petersons own puppy—Buddy.

"I still wish Buddy could have come with us,"

Charles said now, thinking about how much he'd like to stroke the white heart-shaped spot on Buddy's brown chest. Buddy loved that.

Mom turned around in her seat so she could see Charles. "We talked about this. Buddy will have lots of fun with Aunt Amanda."

Aunt Amanda ran a doggie daycare, and she always had extra dogs staying with her overnight, too. When the Petersons went away, they let Buddy stay with her. Buddy loved playing with the other dogs. Charles knew it really was a treat for Buddy, but he also knew he would really miss his favorite puppy. He would miss petting him, and playing with him, and lying on the couch with him. He would miss—well, everything.

"Besides, the place we are staying isn't like the last time," Mom went on now. "It's a bed and breakfast. It's in a big house, but it's more like a hotel."

"Buddy wouldn't really feel at home," Dad said. 'The person who owns the house lives right there, so it's not like we're at our own house."

"But the owner will cook us breakfast, right?" Lizzie added. "Good breakfasts. Like pancakes and muffins." Charles was surprised that Lizzie was thinking about food. Didn't she miss Buddy, too?

"Yes," Mom said. "And we can get take-out for dinner. It's a real vacation when Dad and I don't have to cook. It gives us more time to be with you."

Dad nodded. "We're going to teach the Bean how to swim."

"Like a dolphin," the Bean said. He scrunched his lips together like he was giving a kiss, making a fish face.